JUDY MOODY AND FRIENDS
A Totally Moody Treasury

Megan McDonald
illustrated by Erwin Madrid
based on the characters
created by Peter H. Reynolds

CANDLEWICK PRESS

First edition in this format 2018

This edition published specially for RMS 2018 by Candlewick Press

Library of Congress Cataloging-in-Publication Data is available for the hardcover editions.

Judy Moody and Friends: Stink Moody in Master of Disaster
Library of Congress Catalog Card Number 2013957338
ISBN 978-0-7636-7218-8 (hardcover)
ISBN 978-0-7636-7447-2 (paperback)

Judy Moody and Friends: Triple Pet Trouble
Library of Congress Catalog Card Number 2014955349
ISBN 978-0-7636-7443-4 (hardcover)
ISBN 978-0-7636-7615-5 (paperback)

Judy Moody and Friends: Not-So-Lucky Lefty
Library of Congress Catalog Card Number 2018935019
ISBN 978-0-7636-9605-4 (hardcover)
ISBN 978-0-7636-9847-8 (paperback)

ISBN 978-1-5362-0493-3 (RMS Edition)

18 APS 1

Printed in Humen, Dongguan, China

This book was typeset in ITC Stone Informal.
The illustrations were created digitally.

Candlewick Press
99 Dover Street
Somerville, Massachusetts 02144

visit us at www.candlewick.com

Stink Moody
in Master of Disaster

CONTENTS

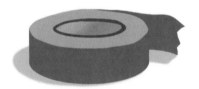

CHAPTER 1
The Sherlock-Holmes Comet

Judy and Stink were sleeping out in the backyard. Judy and Stink were stargazing. Judy and Stink were searching the sky for comet P/2015 OZ4. The Sherman-Holm comet. Stink called it the Sherlock-Holmes comet.

The night sky looked like the *Starry Night* painting, only better. "No blinking, Stink," Judy told him.

"A comet is a once-in-a-lifetime thing. No way would you want to miss it."

Stink tried not to blink. But thinking about blinking just made him blinkier.

"Sure is dark out here," said Stink.

"That's because it's nighttime, Stink."

"Sure is quiet out here," said Stink.

"That's because it's nighttime, Stink."

Judy pointed to a band of stars that looked like a giant brushstroke across the sky. "That's the Milky Way," said Judy.

"Hey! There's the Big Dipper. And the Little Dipper. And the Medium Dipper."

"And there's Wynken, Blynken, and Nod," said Judy.

"For real?" asked Stink.

"Gotcha!" said Judy, laughing herself silly.

It was dark for a long time. It was quiet for a long time.

9

"They should call this star-*waiting*," said Stink.

"Good things come to those who wait, Stink."

"Says who?"

"Abe Lincoln. The ketchup bottle. Mom and Dad."

While he waited, Stink dumped out his backpack. "Star book. Star map. Star finder. Flashlight. Toilet-paper-tube telescope, and . . . my Star Talker DL7."

Stink pressed a button.

"The full moon in March is called a Worm Moon."

Stink pressed the button again.

"A star in Draco, the Dragon, was used by ancient Egyptians to build pyramids."

Stink pressed the button again.

"The full moon in March is called a Worm Moon."

Stink pressed the button again.

"The full moon in March is called a Worm Moon."

Judy put her hands over her ears. "Make that thing stop! All you need for stargazing is your eyes, Stink. And a little P and Q."

"P and Q?"

"Peace and quiet."

12

Stink opened his *Big Head Book of Stars.* Stink held his star map up to the sky. He turned it this way and that.

Judy watched the twinkling stars in the velvet sky and waited.

Stink spun his star finder to August.

Stink squinted one eye and looked through his toilet-paper-tube telescope.

Stink studied his star map. He
found the Eagle,

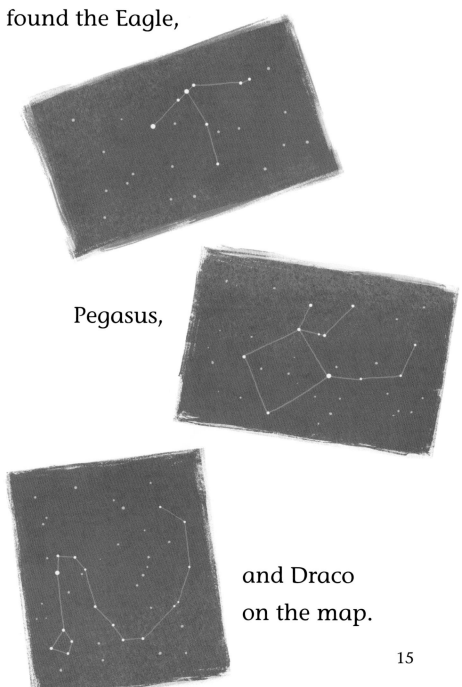

Pegasus,

and Draco
on the map.

Judy studied the night sky. She found the Swan, the tail of Scorpius, and the Summer Triangle in the sky. Then she saw . . . a flash of light. A giant ball of fire streaked across the inky sky faster than a wink! Faster than a blink.

Judy jumped up. "Stink? Did you . . . did you see that?"

Stink looked up from his map. "See what?"

"The comet! I think Sherlock-Holmes just flew across the sky!"

"I missed it?" Stink wailed. "Wait. What did it look like?"

"Like a red-hot freaky fireball streaking across the sky. Like Fourth of July fireworks. Like five thousand shooting stars."

"No way did you see a comet," said Stink. "Comets are made of ice, not fire. They don't streak across the sky. And a comet has a tail. Did it have a tail?"

Judy shrugged.

"It was probably just a shooting star or a meteor or a fireball or a supernova."

"Or a UFO!" Judy teased.

"Whatever it was, maybe it'll go by again!" Stink said hopefully.

"It will," said Judy. "In about a hundred years."

"A hundred years! I can't wait till I'm a hundred and seven!"

Judy got an idea. "Stink, I know how you can see a comet." She crawled inside the T. P. Club tent. "Don't come in until I say so."

Stink waited for what felt like a hundred and seven years. "Can I come in yet?"

"Not yet."

Stink itched and scratched and waited. "Now?"

"Not yet."

"How about now?"

"No!"

"Did you know the full moon in March is called a Worm Moon?" Stink asked.

Silence.

"There sure is a lot of peace and quiet out here," said Stink.

"You can come in now," said Judy.

Finally! Stink crawled into the tent.
The inside was covered with stars—
glow-in-the-dark star stickers.

"Wow!" Stink gazed up at his own
small sky. "There's the Big Dipper!
And the Little Dipper. Even the
Medium Dipper!"

Judy pointed to a three-star cluster.

"This is Wynken, Blynken, and Nod. And that's not all," said Judy. She turned on not one but two flashlights. One made a fuzzy ball on the tent sky. She held the other flashlight at an angle to make a tail.

"It's a comet!" said Stink. "The Sherlock-Holmes comet!"

When Judy's arms got tired, she turned off the flashlights and crawled inside her sleeping bag. "Show's over. I'm going to bed."

"I didn't get to see the real comet," said Stink, "but I got the next best thing. My own private galaxy. Thanks, Judy."

"Mm-hmm," said a sleepy Judy.

Stink opened the tent flap to peek at the real sky one last time. The stars twinkled like glitter. All of a sudden, a star streaked across the sky.

"A shooting star!" said Stink. "I saw one! For real!"

"Make a wish," mumbled Judy.

Stink closed his eyes and made a wish.

That night, Stink and Judy went to the Land of Nod under the winking, blinking stars. If Stink's wish came true, they would be doing the exact same thing in another hundred years.

CHAPTER 2
Master of Disaster

Stink raced home from Saturday Science Club. "The sky is falling! The sky is falling!"

Judy looked up from her ant habitat. "Slow down, Chicken Little," said Judy. "What are you saying?"

"The asteroids are coming! The asteroids are coming! I just found out that a giant meteorite landed in

Russia. No lie. And an even bigger one might be headed for Earth."

"Don't worry, Stink. Dad says tons of space junk hits Earth every day."

"*Don't worry?* Tell that to the dinosaurs. There could be a rock out there with *your* name on it. It could be speeding toward Earth right now, going sixty miles per second. *Disaster*oid!"

Judy watched an ant dig a tunnel.

"How can you think about ants at a time like this?" Stink cried. "Any minute you could be squashed like a pancake. Or squished right down to the size of . . . an ant!"

"Ooh, I could be a yellow crazy ant," said Judy. "And you could be an odorous ant. Odorous ants smell like rotting coconuts when you squish them."

"Get serious," said Stink.

"Stink, if an asteroid hits Earth—"

"You said *if*. But it's not *if*, Judy. It's *when*."

"What can *I* do about it?" asked Judy.

"You can build a net the size of Virginia to catch the asteroid. You can invent an anti-asteroid Blast-o-Matic machine to destroy it before it reaches us. *Blast*eroid!"

"That sounds too much like homework," said Judy.

"*I'm* going to make an asteroid-proof bunker in the basement."

"You hate the basement," said Judy. "Dark. Scary. Spiders."

"I'd rather be bitten by ten hundred spiders than squished to the size of a coconut ant by a killer asteroid."

Stink put on his bike helmet, water wings, and knee pads. He made himself an aluminum-foil cape. *Asteroid Boy!* Asteroid Boy would protect Earth from killer asteroids!

Stink carried a blanket, a flashlight, and a light saber down to the basement. He carried Toady the toad and Astro the guinea pig to the basement. He carried half his room to the basement. He even took the toaster to the basement.

"Mom! Dad!" called Judy. "Stink just moved into the basement."

"He hates the basement," said Mom.

"That's what I said," said Judy.

"Why the basement?" asked Dad.

"To hide from killer asteroids," said Judy. "They're speeding toward Earth this very second."

"Tons of space junk hits Earth every day," said Dad.

"That's what I said you said," said Judy.

"He'll change his mind at the first sign of a spider," said Mom.

"He'll change his mind as soon as it gets dark," said Dad.

Judy and Mouse the cat tiptoed down the stairs to the stinky basement. Stink had built a fort out of boxes and boards, chairs and crates.

"Like my bunker?" Stink asked.
Before Judy could answer, a loud
roaring sound came from outside.
"Did you hear that? A sonic boom!"
"Lawn mower," said Judy.
Next they heard a whooshing
sound.

"Did you hear that?" said Stink. "A space storm!"

"Washing machine," said Judy.

Stink heard a crash like breaking glass.

"It's here!" Stink cried. "The asteroid has landed!"

"That was Dad. Doing dishes again," said Judy.

"Do you feel hot?" Stink asked. "I feel hot." He peered out the window. "Did the house just shake? Is that a radioactive glow?"

Just then, the lights went out. The basement went dark. Dark as an eclipse. Dark as a black hole.

"This is it! Killer asteroid hits Earth and takes out power grid!" Stink threw on a pair of goggles, grabbed his light saber, and yelled, "Never fear! Asteroid Boy is here!" He pointed to the toaster, which was covered with magnets. "Judy, activate the Anti-Asteroid Magnetic-Repulsion Device!"

"Stink, I think *you're* the asteroid. You have too much stuff plugged in down here. You blew a fuse. Dad's going to blow a fuse, too."

"But . . . we're alive!" said Stink. He fell to his knees in relief. "We survived a giant ball of rock, metal, and dust crashing into Earth at sixty thousand miles per second."

Judy sniffed the air. "I don't smell rotting coconuts. So I guess we didn't get squashed like ants."

Stink ran outside. Judy ran after him.

Stink peered up at the sky with his asteroid-proof X-ray-vision goggles. Stink peered up into the trees. Stink peered down at the grass.

"I need proof," said Stink. "Proof that I survived an asteroid hitting Earth faster than a speeding bullet."

"You're proof, Stink. I'm proof. See? We're not as flat as pancakes."

"Pancakes! That reminds me. I'm hungry."

"Surviving an asteroid attack will do that," said Judy. "Let's ask Mom if she'll make us silver-dollar pancakes."

"*When*," said Stink.

"Huh?"

"Not *if*. *When*. Ask Mom *when* she's going to make us pancakes."

"Stink, you are the Master of Disaster!" said Judy. "If an asteroid ever hits Earth, I'm calling Asteroid Boy."

"Not *if*," said Asteroid Boy, grinning ear to ear. "*When.*"

CHAPTER 3
Albert Einstink

PLOP! A big fat envelope landed on the Moodys' front step.

"It's for me!" said Stink.

"It's for me!" said Judy.

"But it has *my* name on it," said Stink.

Judy stared at the big fat envelope. It was not her mail-order ants.

Stink grabbed the envelope and

tore it open. "It's from the way-official Name-That-Star Company."

"Name-the-What?"

"Name-That-Star. I'm going to have a star named after me."

"Stink, there are a million, billion stars in the galaxy. I don't think they're going to name one for you."

"Yah-huh." He held up the papers. "It's all right here in my star-naming kit. There's a way-official certificate.

Way-official instructions.

And a real-and-actual
photo of my very own
star."

Judy studied the star photo. "Huh. What are you going to name it? *Stink Star?*" She cracked up.

Stink's jaw dropped. "Oh, no," he moaned. "I never thought of that. The Stink Star is not a very good name for a star."

"Use your real name. Call it the James Star."

"*James* is not special enough for a star. There are three Jameses in my second-grade class!"

Judy picked up her Grouchy pencil. "I'll help you. You make a list of names, and I'll make a list of names. Then you'll have tons of names to choose from."

Stink thought and thought. Stink chewed his pencil.

Judy scribbled on her list. "Stella? Stellina? Starla?" she read.

"No girl names," said Stink.

"Orion? Sirius? Hercules?"

"Taken," said Stink.

"Balthazar?"

"Balthazar Moody," said Stink. "Maybe."

Big Head Book of Baby Names

"Let's hear some names on your list," said Judy.

"Batman? Superman? Plutoman?"

"Superman Moody? No way. There's kryptonite in outer space, you know. Your star would get clobbered."

"Spike? Dracula? Godzilla?" Stink asked.

"Dracula Moody. I like it!" said Judy. "But it would starve up there."

Stink got out the *Big Head Book of Baby Names*. "Maybe I'll find a name in here!" He opened to the *A*'s. "Abner, Achilles, Achoo," Stink read.

"Bless you," said Judy.

"No, that's a name: Achoo!"

"No way is somebody named Achoo," said Judy.

Stink frowned. "You're right. My star can't be named for a sneeze."

He flipped some pages. "Sheesh. There are ten hundred names in here. It will take light-years to find the right name."

"Close your eyes, open the book, and point," said Judy.

Stink closed his eyes. Stink opened the book. Stink pointed. "Lollipop,"

he read. "Ten thousand names and I point to the name of a big slobbery sucker?"

Stink went to find Mom and Dad. He asked them how to choose a brand-new, not-sneezy, un-slobbery-sucker name to put on a star.

"A name should say something about you," said Mom.

"Like Judy is moody? And Riley Rottenberger is rotten?" asked Stink.

"Sort of," said Dad.

"And like Stink is stinky?" said Judy.

"Try thinking of something that makes you special," said Dad. "Or someone you admire."

Stink's face lit up. "I got it! Albert Einstink!"

"Forget it, Stink Face," said Judy.
"Your brain is way too puny."

"How about my initials and my birthday: JEM-229."

"My brother, the robot," said Judy.

"How about a super-cool spy name, like Mosquito? Or Neptune Shadow?"

"That's it!" said Judy.

"Really?"

"N-O!" said Judy. "Let's put all the names in a bowl, Stink. We'll mix them up. Then close your eyes, reach in, and pull one out."

"Hey! You just gave me an idea," said Stink. He scribbled in his notebook. "Ready for this?"

"Ready, Freddy!" said Judy. "Hercules-Balthazar-Superman-Dracula-Achoo-Lollipop-JEM-229-Mosquito-Albert-Einstink."

"You're going to name your star Hercules-Balthazar-Superman-Dracula-Achoo-Lollipop-JEM-229-Mosquito-Albert-Einstink?"

"Right."

Judy picked up the way-official star packet. She read silently for about a hundred light-years. Then she said, "Stink, there are rules. First of all, a star name can't be more than sixteen letters long. The name you picked is like sixteen million letters long. Plus some numbers!"

"Yikes," said Stink.

"Second of all, a star name can only be one word. Your name is nine million words long."

"Double yikes," said Stink. He scratched his head.

HOW TO
NAME THAT STAR
in 50 Easy

"I know!" he said. "How about if my star's name is Hercules-Balthazar-Superman-Dracula-Achoo-Lollipop-JEM-229-Mosquito-Albert-Einstink, but you call it Stink for short?"

"Perfect," said Mom and Dad.

"You think?" asked Stink.

"If the Stink fits, wear it," said Judy.

Triple Pet Trouble

For the helpful crew at California Carnivores

M. M.

To my wife, Hoài

E. M.

CONTENTS

CHAPTER 1
Jaws in Love

Jaws looked droopy. Jaws looked mopey. Jaws looked wilty. Jaws was Judy Moody's Venus flytrap. Two of his leaves were turning black. One of his traps was turning dead.

Judy Moody stuck her Grouchy pencil in one of his traps and . . . *snap . . . trap . . . NOT!* Jaws did not snap his trap. Not even when she tried an ant, a tiny cricket, or a roly-poly.

Stink's jaw dropped when he saw Judy's pet. "What's wrong with Jaws? He looks like moldy old bread."

"He's sick," said Judy.

"Ooh. Maybe he has the measles."

"I don't get it," said Judy. "I feed him earwigs from Dad's garden. I take him outside in winter. I snip off his dead leaves when they turn black."

"Maybe he doesn't like his new haircut," said Stink.

"I know," said Judy. "Dr. Judy, Pet Vet, to the rescue!"

Dr. Judy gave Jaws a bath—with rainwater.

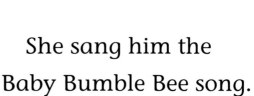

She sang him the Baby Bumble Bee song.

She read to him from *Charlotte's Web*.

72

"Don't read him a sad book!" said Stink.

"It's his favorite," said Judy. But Jaws looked as droopy as ever.

Judy looked stuff up in her *Big Head Book of Bug-Eating Plants*. "It says here that there's only one place in the world where Venus flytraps grow in nature."

"Where?"

"A place called Cape Fear," said Judy, "in North Carolina."

Stink shivered. The Moodys' cat, Mouse, pulled her toy mouse in closer. "Maybe Jaws is homesick," said Stink.

"Maybe Jaws is just lonely," Judy said.

"Aha! Jaws needs a friend," said Stink. He ran downstairs and came back carrying a fishbowl. A goldfish was floating on top of the sloshing water.

Stink set the bowl down next to Jaws. "Jaws, meet your new friend, Goldilocks."

Judy peered into the bowl. "Stink. That's no goldfish. That's a cracker. A goldfish-shaped cracker."

"Jaws doesn't know that," whispered Stink.

"He'd probably rather *eat* than *meet* his new friend," Judy whispered back.

Jaws did not perk up one bit.

"It's not working," said Stink.

"Making friends takes time," said Judy.

Judy and Stink gave it time.
One day. Two days. Three days.
Judy peered into the goldfish bowl.
"Goldilocks looks puffy," said Judy,
"and pale."

"Let me see," said Stink, pulling the
fishbowl toward him. The cracker fell
to pieces. "Argh! Jaws's new friend
just became five friends!" cried Stink.

"Jaws looks worse," said Judy.

"You'd look bad, too, if your best friend just turned into Cream of Goldfish," said Stink.

"Let's move Jaws over to the window," said Judy. "I think he needs more light."

They set Jaws down on the window seat next to Mouse and a pile of papers and junk. "Move over, Mouse," said Judy. "Make way for Jaws."

Mouse leaped to the floor, but a piece of paper got stuck to her paw. Junk mail! Mouse shook her paw, trying to get rid of it.

"Mouse is trying to show us something," said Stink.

Judy unstuck the piece of junk mail from Mouse's paw. On the flyer were pictures of a Venus flytrap, a pitcher plant, a sundew, and a cobra lily. *Carnivore city!*

The flyer said GRAND OPENING! The flyer said that a store called Cape Fear Carnivores was opening right there in Frog Neck Lake!

Judy kissed her cat on the nose. She, Dr. Judy Moody, knew just what to do to save Jaws.

Judy and her dad took Jaws to Cape Fear Carnivores. Judy talked to the owner, Peter Tomato. Peter Tomato knew everything in the world about bug-eating plants.

Peter Tomato helped Judy start her very own bog. First she picked out a pot that looked like a mini bathtub. Next she filled it with sand and peat moss. Then she planted Jaws in the bog next to a brand-new, way-tall, red-and-green North American pitcher plant.

"Jaws," said Judy, "meet Petunia, your new bug-eating buddy!"

When Judy and Jaws and Petunia got home, Stink peered into one of the pitcher plant's long tubes.

"There's water in there," said Stink, "and a dead fly."

"That's how a pitcher plant traps its food," said Judy. "An insect smells nectar, lands on the mouth of the plant, and—*zoom*—falls right down into the tube."

"Cool," said Stink.

"Did you know some pitcher plants eat animal poop? They like shrew poo."

"Hardee-har-har," said Stink. "You made that up."

"Did not!" said Judy. "Peter Tomato at Cape Fear Carnivores told me. Peter Tomato would not lie."

Judy sat back to admire her bog. Jaws did not look droopy or mopey or wilty. Jaws looked positively perky.

At last, Jaws had company. He curled a leaf around Petunia, the pitcher plant.

"Look," said Judy. "I think Jaws is in love!"

"Love at first sight," said Stink.

"Love at first bite," said Judy.

CHAPTER 2
Mystic Mouse

Judy was reading to Mouse from her *Big Head Book of Pets.* She was reading all about parrots and potbellied pigs and pocket pets—pets that can fit in a pocket.

Then she looked out the window. "Check it out, Mouse. Stink has a lemonade stand. And his lemonade stand has a big long line."

Jingle-jangle. "I can already hear the jingle of all the quarters in Stink's pockets."

All of a sudden, she, Judy Moody, had an idea. A pockets-full-of-quarters idea.

She set up a table down the sidewalk from Stink. She hung up a sign. She put out an empty jar. She hid her *Big Head Book of Pets* under the table, just in case.

"Hey!" said Stink. "This is my corner."

"It's a free country, Stink."

"Why is Mouse wearing a turban and sitting on your mood pillow like a queen?"

PET PSYCHIC:
Mouse the
Mind Reader

Judy pointed to her sign. PET
PSYCHIC: MOUSE THE MIND READER.
"Mouse knows what other pets are
thinking. She knew Jaws needed a
friend, remember?"

"What's the jar for?"

"The jar is for when all the quarters
start to roll in. Twenty-five cents a
reading."

Stink went back to his table. "Ice-cold lemonade!" cried Stink. "Hand-stirred. Only twenty-five cents!"

"Meet pet psychic Mouse Moody!" called Judy. "Got a pet problem? Mouse can solve it!"

Kids gawked at Mouse on their way to get lemonade but didn't stop. Judy put up more signs. FREE TUMMY RUBS! FREE HEAD SCRATCHES!

FREE TUMMY RUBS!

PET PSYCHIC: Mouse the Mind Reader

Rocky was first in line. "Hi, Rock," said Judy. "What's your pet problem?"

Rocky held out his pet iguana. "It's Houdini. He turned a weird color. And his skin is peeling."

Judy ducked under the table to peek at her Big Head book in secret. She sprang back up and leaned over her cat. "Mouse the Mind Reader

FREE
HEAD
SCRATCHES!

has spoken. She says Houdini is just growing. That's why he's shedding his skin." Judy scratched the back of the iguana's head. "Give him a nice bath, mist him every morning, and he'll feel better."

"Thanks!" said Rocky.

"Twenty-five cents, please," said Judy. *Ka-ching!*

© 2015 MM & PHR

© 2015 MM & PHR

© 2015 MM & PHR

"She's not sleeping. She's thinking," said Judy, putting her ear up to Mouse.

"Mouse the Magnificent says it's all about the treats. Do a fun trick with Cookie, but let *your sister* give her a treat."

"Mouse told you all that?" said Frank. "Wow!" He dropped a quarter in the jar.

FREE HEAD SCRATCHES!

Next in line were Amy Namey and Jessica Finch. "I don't have a pet," said Amy.

Mouse curled her tail into a question mark. Judy said, "Mouse the Magnificent says, How about a pocket pet? Sugar gliders are cute. They fit in your pocket. Or a goldfish. *Not* the cracker kind. Twenty-five cents, please."

"But I'm not here about a pet for me," said Amy. "I'm here about PeeGee." She pointed to Jessica Finch's potbellied pig on a leash.

"PeeGee is freaking out," Jessica told Judy. "Every time he comes into my room, he knocks over my chair and chews my shoes and squeals like a—"

"Pig?" asked Judy.

Jessica nodded.

"Got that, Mouse?" Judy said. Mouse purred. Mouse purred some more.

"Mouse is thinking," said Judy.

"How do you know what she's thinking?" asked Jessica.

"Mouse and I are of one mind. It sounds to me—I mean to Mouse—like *somebody* needs to learn a few rules at obedience school."

"I love rules!" said Jessica. "And obedience. Maybe I can teach PeeGee myself."

Clink. Clink. Clink-clink-clink. The quarters kept on coming.

Mouse helped a parakeet with no tweet (Hello! Turn on the light),

a fish with ick, a.k.a. measles (Hello! Get fish medicine from the pet store),

and a pet rock that lost one googly
eye (Hello, glue!).

Mouse was a regular Dr. Dolittle,
an animal whisperer of the third
kind, a pet psychic with a sixth sense.

Judy jingled and jangled the
quarters in her jar for Stink to hear.

"Hey!" said Stink. "You're stealing
all my customers. Everybody wants
to see Mouse the Mystic. Nobody's
thirsty anymore."

Judy held up Mouse's water bowl for everyone to see. "Mouse the Mystic will now gaze into the Eternal Water Bowl of Serenity."

FREE
TUMMY
RUBS!

PET PSYCHIC:
Mouse the
Reader

FREE
HEAD
SCRATCHES!

Mouse twitched her whiskers. Mouse licked her lips. "Mouse feels a great thirst coming on," said Judy.

Mouse stuck out her tongue and lapped up water like crazy.

A hush fell over the crowd. Everyone gazed at Mouse the Mind Reader.

"Come to think of it," said Frank, "I feel thirsty, too."

"Me, too," said Rocky and Amy at the same time.

"Me, three," said Jessica Finch. "PeeGee's thirsty, too."

Now everybody rushed to get in line at Stink's table. In two minutes flat, Stink ran out of lemonade. He ran into the house and came back carrying a pitcher of water.

"Ice-cold water!" Stink yelled. "From the Eternal Fountain of Thirst Quenching. Hand-stirred! Only twenty-five cents a cup!"

CHAPTER 3
Toady and the Vampire

Zing! Toady zinged off Judy's bottom bunk bed. *Boing!* He boinged off her finger-knitting yarn. Stink's pet toad, Toady, was going nutso, zinging and boinging all over the place.

Judy scooped him up, then squished into her window seat between Mouse and the bog buddies, Jaws and Petunia.

EEW! All of a sudden, Judy felt something warm and wet in her hand. *Gross-o-rama!* She set the toad down.

Toady made a puddle on her mood pillow. "Bad Toady!" Judy said.

Then he made a puddle on top of her gumball machine. "Bad, bad Toady!" Judy said.

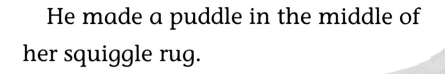
He made a puddle in the middle of her squiggle rug.

"That does it!" said Judy. "You and I are going on a field trip."

Judy rode Toady to Jessica Finch's house on her bike. A sign in the yard said JESSICA FINCH'S DOGGY DAY CARE AND OBEDIENCE SCHOOL.

JESSICA FINCH'S
DOGGY
DAY CARE
AND
OBEDIENCE
SCHOOL

Judy did not see a single dog. She did see Houdini, Rocky's iguana; Cookie, Frank's parrot; and PeeGee WeeGee, Jessica's pig, running around like crazy. Jessica was shouting, "Sit," "Stay," and "Heel," but none of them listened. None of them behaved.

This looked more like DIS-obedience school!

Jessica Finch and Amy Namey ran over to Judy. A stripe-faced fur ball with dark eyes and a pink nose stuck its head out of Amy's pocket. "Meet Boo," said Amy. "It's short for Peek-a-Boo."

"You got a sugar glider?" asked Judy. "You lucky dog!"

"How come *you're* here?" Jessica asked Judy.

"Toady's being a bad toad today." Judy told them about the toad pee on everything. "Will you take one more student?"

Jessica frowned. Jessica hemmed and hawed.

"Don't be a toadstool," said Judy.

"Okay. He can stay."

"Sit!" Jessica said to the animals. Houdini crawled away.

"Sit!" Jessica said again. Cookie hopped up and down and clacked her beak.

"Sit!" PeeGee just chased his tail.

"Sit!" Boo jumped out of Amy's pocket and knocked over his barrel of toy monkeys.

"Sit!" said Jessica. Toady sat.

Judy clapped her hands. "Toady!
You did it!"

"Stay!" said Jessica. Houdini crawled under a pile of leaves.

"Stay!" Jessica called again. Cookie flapped her wings and flew onto Judy's head.

"Stay!" PeeGee chased his tail some more.

"Stay!" Boo glided through the air and landed on PeeGee.

"Stay!" Jessica told Toady. Toady stayed.

"Good Toady!" Judy yelled.

Jessica held up a Hula-Hoop.
"Jump!" she said. PeeGee
chased after a ball. "Bad pig!"
yelled Jessica. Boo chased
after PeeGee. Cookie chased
after Boo.

Jessica tried again. "Jump!"
Toady jumped . . . right
through the Hula-Hoop!

"You're good at getting Toady to obey," said Judy.

"Gold star for you, Toady." Jessica held him in her hand. "I still want to be in your Toad Pee Club," she said to the toad, "but you won't even pee on me."

"Toady gets an A-plus for Toad School," said Judy.

"That'll be one dollar," said Jessica Finch.

"Will you take four quarters?" Judy asked.

The next day, Judy teased Toady about obedience school. "You are *toadally* teacher's pet!" she said. All of a sudden, she felt something warm and wet on her hand. *Eew!* That naughty toad sprang out of her hand and hopped under the bed.

Judy heard a voice. "Hey, Judy! Want to go monster hunting?" It was Amy Namey.

"I *am* monster hunting," said Judy. She rescued Toady and dusted him off. "*This* monster. Toady acted perfect at obedience school. But the second I got him home, he turned into a little monster again. I don't get it."

Amy wasn't listening. Amy was staring. Amy was pointing at Judy's

new plant on the window seat. "You have a pitcher plant? I saw one in Borneo. It had one of those long scary names like *Carnivoria vampira* or something."

"This isn't a vampire," said Judy. "This is a new friend for Jaws. Her name is Petunia."

"Uh-oh," said Amy.

"What-oh?" asked Judy. She set Toady down on her top bunk.

"Um, I hate to tell you this, but . . . some giant pitcher plants can eat a frog."

Judy sprang up. *A frog-eating pitcher plant? Gulp!*

"Or a mouse or a rat," said Amy, "or a . . . *toad!*"

"No wonder Toady's been acting psycho," said Judy. "He's scared of Petunia, the vampire pitcher plant!"

Judy turned to look at Toady—
Wait! Toady? Where was that toad now?

Judy rushed over to Petunia. "Open wide and say 'Ahh'!" Judy said in her best doctor voice. She looked down Petunia's throat.

Judy did not see a bug. She did not see a spider, ant, or earwig. She saw a puddle. A small puddle of liquid. Amy saw it, too.

Was it . . . could it be . . . toad pee?

"ROAR!" said Judy. "The vampire plant ate Toady!"

Just then, Stink came running into 
Judy's room. "*Who* ate
Toady?" he asked.

"Nobody."

"Where is he,
then?"

"Um . . ." said
Judy.

Just then,
Toady hopped
from the
bedpost to the
desk to the
doorknob.

"Right there," said Amy, pointing.

Stink scooped him up. "Phew. Don't scare me like that."

Judy pushed Stink and Toady toward the door. "Stink! Get him out of here! My room is now officially a FROG-FREE zone."

"A toad is not a frog," said Stink.

"Tell that to the *Toadivoria vampira*!" said Judy.

"The *toadi*-huh?"

Judy pointed to the pitcher plant. "Stink, I hate to tell you this. But Jaws's new BFF is a freaky, frog-eating vampire. No lie. Say hello to Count Petunia."

Not-So-Lucky Lefty

For all the lucky lefties

M. M.

To my wife, Hoài

E. M.

CONTENTS

CHAPTER 1
Lucky Lefty and Mighty Righty

"One, two, three, four, I declare a thumb war." Stink dipped his thumb. He was too quick; Judy couldn't catch him.

Her little brother sure was good at thumb-wrestling. Judy just had to beat him. "Tell me again why I have to do this left-handed?" Judy asked.

"Tomorrow is August thirteenth. If you want to celebrate Left Handers Day with me and Dad," said Stink, "you have to beat me like a southpaw. That means left-handed."

Judy dipped, dived, and dodged Stink's thumb.

Sneak attack! All of a sudden, Stink faked her out, slid his thumb sideways, then—*ka-blam*—pinned her thumb down.

"I win! I win!" Stink spun around the room. "Winner, winner, chicken dinner!"

Wait just a southpaw second. "You have to hold my thumb down for three seconds," said Judy. "That was not three seconds."

"Was too," said Stink. "I beat you fair and square with Lucky Lefty here."

Judy wiggled her right hand. "I could beat you thumbs-down if you let me use Mighty Righty."

"You mean the right hand of doom? Lefties rule all!"

"What's so great about being left-handed, anyway?" Judy asked.

"Left-handers are creative. Left-handers are geniuses. Left-handers are presidents! Einstein was a lefty. Kermit the Frog is a lefty. Half of all cats are lefties."

Mouse batted her squeak toy with her left paw. *Traitor!* Even Judy's cat was left-handed.

Judy was feeling left out.

Judy wanted to be creative. Judy wanted to be a genius. Judy wanted to be a president. But most of all, Judy wanted to go with Stink and Dad on their Left Handers Day visit to the pretzel factory.

"C'mon, Stink," said Judy. "Give me another chance."

"Okay, here's a test."

"What kind of test?" asked Judy.

"Scratch your nose," said Stink.

Judy scratched her nose.

"Open the door," said Stink. Judy opened the door.

"Write your name," said Stink. Judy wrote her name.

"High five!" said Stink. Judy high-fived Stink.

"Your test is complete," said Stink.

"That's it? Awesome! I get an A for *Amazing!*"

"You get an F for *Flunked*. You used your right hand every single time. You even high-fived me with your right hand of doom."

"ROAR!" said Judy. "You tricked me."

"See? Being left-handed is harder than you think," said Stink.

"I just need a little practice."

Stink sighed and handed Judy
a piece of paper and a pair of left-
handed scissors. "Let's see you cut out
a circle with your left hand."

"Easy-peasy mac-and-cheesy," said
Judy. But it was not so easy-peasy. Her
left hand wouldn't behave. She felt
like a preschooler. She held up her
circle at last. *GULP!*

"Was your circle chewed by a great white shark or something?" Stink asked.

"Or something."

Judy read Stink's T-shirt: LIVE LIFE LEFT. She tried to write it on one of her old T-shirts with her left hand. It looked like LOVE LAF LEAF.

"See?" said Judy. "I can do stuff left-handed."

"Fine," said Stink, "you can come with me and Dad to It's Raining Pretzels tomorrow on one condition: you have to be left-handed the whole entire day."

Judy did not want to be left out. Judy wanted to have triple fun with Stink and Dad.

"You're on." Judy raised her left hand in the air. "I, Judy Moody, do solemnly swear to be left-handed for one whole entire day."

CHAPTER 2
Pretzilla

The next morning, Judy opened her left eye.

Happy Left Handers Day!

Judy brushed her hair left-handed. She looked like an electric eel. Judy brushed her teeth left-handed. She got toothpaste up her nose. Judy pulled on her shirt left-handed. She fell flat on the floor.

Yikes. At this rate, Judy was not going to be president of the Creative Geniuses and Cats Club any time soon.

"All aboard the Lefty Express," called Dad.

Judy raced Stink to the car. *Oops!*
She *almost* opened the door with her
right hand.

She tried to buckle her seat belt left-
handed, but she got as twisted up as
an octopus in an ocean of yarn.

"Help!"

Stink untwisted her.

Judy smoothed out her shirt. All
the way to It's Raining Pretzels, Judy
squeezed a ball in her left hand.
Open, shut, open, shut.

"What are you doing?" Stink asked.
"Making my left hand stronger,"
said Judy.

At the shop, there were pretzel rods, sticks, and twists. Blue pretzels, frozen pretzels, mustache pretzels, pretzels that spelled words. A sign said THE WORLD'S BIGGEST PRETZEL WEIGHS 1,728 POUNDS!

"How about a snack first," said
Dad. "Hot dogs in pretzel buns?"

"And hot cocoa," said Stink. "We
can dip our pretzels."

Judy went to reach for a green
Alien Pretzel. Stink held his pretzel
mustache under his nose. "Pretzel

police! You're under arrest for using your right hand."

Judy stopped just in time. *Phew!* That was a close one. She raised her *left* hand. "I solemnly swear to obey the Law of the Left for the rest of the day."

When Judy used her left hand to squeeze ketchup on her hot dog, it squirted all over her.

"You look like a zombie!" Stink cried.

When Judy took a bite of hot dog, it shot out of the bun and landed in Stink's lap.

When Judy tried to pick up her
cocoa left-handed, she knocked it
over.

After their snack, Judy and Stink went on a pretzel hunt. They made their own pretzels. They even played pretzel Twister.

"Hey, look," said Dad, pointing to the activity room. "Who wants to build a pretzel roller coaster?"

"Last one there is pickled pretzel poop!" called Stink.

Tables with bowls of pretzels lined the room.

"Let's make our coaster shaped like an upside-down pretzel," said Judy.

Dad sketched it on a napkin.

"Here's a double-reverse coaster . . ."

"With bat wings," added Stink.

Judy and Stink worked on a ramp made of mini-waffle pretzels. Dad used pretzel rods to hold up the first loop. Judy tried to add a pretzel to the loop. *Oops-a-daisy!* She bumped Stink, making him knock over the ramp.

"You wrecked it!" cried Stink.

"Me? *You* wrecked it," said Judy.

"*You* bumped *me*," said Stink.

"Stink, how about if we let Judy use her right hand for this?" said Dad.

"NO!" said Judy. "I have to be a lefty *all day*."

"Then no more fighting," said Dad.

"I'll do the pretzels," Stink said to Judy. "You stick to the glue."

Judy picked up the glue. She tried to make a dot. It came out a blob. She tried to make a line. It came out a glob. She tried to make a squiggle. It came out a giant gloopy glob of goop!

For the next hour, Judy and Stink stacked pretzels every which way.

Their coaster was more glue than pretzel.

"Pretzilla!" said Stink.

"*Glue*-zilla!" said Judy.

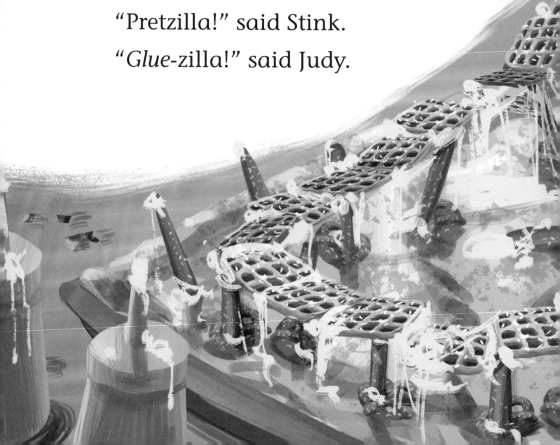

Judy, Stink, and Dad went around admiring the other pretzel coasters. When they got back to their table, Pretzilla had a ribbon on its name tag.

"We won?!" cried Stink.

"Each coaster gets a special ribbon," said Dad.

"What did we win for?" asked Judy. "Most glue?"

"Most creative name," said Dad.

"Lefties rule!" cried Stink.

"Yeah we do," said Judy. She high-fived Stink and Dad with her left hand.

Dad waved tickets in the air. "For making a coaster, we get free passes to play goony golf."

"Can we, can we, can we?" asked Judy and Stink.

"Let's go!" said Dad.

CHAPTER 3
The Ultimate Left-Handed, High-Flying Hole in One

Judy, Stink, and Dad sang all the way to the goony-golf place. They sang the purple people eater song at the top of their lungs.

Stink saw it first. "There it is!" The giant purple-people-eater statue greeted them in front of the mini-golf course.

"The purple people eater's still here!" said Dad. "Do you kids know that this is where I brought Mom on our first date?"

"For real?" asked Judy.

"No way!" said Stink.

"True story," said Dad. "We played glow-in-the-dark goony golf till midnight and sipped a root-beer float from the same straw."

"Gross!" said Stink.

Stink asked for an orange left-handed golf club. "My putter is called The Orange Crush because I am so going to crush you."

Judy made a face. Dad chose a blue club. "Why don't you get a right-handed putter, Judy?"

"The day isn't over. I can't give up on being a lefty now." Judy picked up a left-handed purple putter.

The goony-golf course was full of windmills and waterfalls, spiderwebs and shipwrecks. When they got to the first green, Stink tapped the ball into the hole in two strokes. "Par two!"

Then Judy was up. Tap. Judy's ball rolled a few inches. Tap. The ball plinked off the edge.

Tap.

Tap.

Tap.

Tap.

Score!

"It took Judy six tries!" cried Stink. "The Orange Crush rules."

"It's hard being a lefty," said Judy.

"It is," agreed Dad, "but you'll get the hang of it."

"Yeah, after about seven years!" said Stink.

Judy swung, swatted, and swooshed her way through the first nine holes. Stink only had to duck twice when Judy's ball zinged sideways.

"The Orange Crush is crushing you!" Stink cried.

They came to the next hole. "This time, hit the ball a little harder," Dad told Judy. "Give it some speed."

Swoosh! Judy's ball went singing through the air and landed—*PLOP*—in the middle of Pirate Pond.

"It's a sinker. You'll have to ask for another ball," called Stink.

Judy slumped. "When is *Right* Handers Day?" she grumped.

"Every single day of the year," Stink and Dad said at the very same time.

"Same-same!" said Judy. She ran off to get a new ball.

When she came back, Stink was on hole thirteen. "Hey, it's my turn," said Judy.

"Nah-uh," said Stink. "You still have to finish the snake hole."

"Stink, let's cut Judy a break," said Dad.

"Yeah, Stinker. This could be my first hole in one."

Stink snorted.

Judy hit the ball hard. The ball sped down the green, soared loop-de-loop through a metal shoot, and spun in circles around the hole.

Judy held her breath. The ball stopped . . . right *next* to the hole.

"Ooh," said Dad. "So close!"

The next hole was a haunted house. Ghosts gave Stink the goose bumps. Skeletons gave Stink the shivers. He skipped ahead and drove his ball through a giant pair of glasses.

"Hey, Cheater Pants," called Judy. "You skipped a hole."

"Haunted houses give me the creeps," said Stink.

"Lefties scare easy," said Judy. "True fact."

"Maybe we do," Dad said, laughing.

"Do not!" called Stink. But he still skipped the haunted house.

Judy putted her way through
a pyramid, a sea monster, and a
Chinese dragon. At last she caught
up to Stink at hole eighteen.

Stink made his last shot. "The Orange Crush is over and out. Dad, can I get a root-beer float?" Dad made his trying-to-decide-if-Stink-can-have-sugar face.

"Like you and Mom," said Stink. "C'mon. It's Left Handers Day!"

Stink ran to the window and came back with a big frothy drink. He slurped it at the picnic table next to hole eighteen.

Dad made the shot in two strokes. "Now you try. Really put your arm into it."

"So I have to hit the ball uphill *and* sink it in one of those holes in the shipwreck?" Judy asked.

"Yes. The last hole's the hardest," said Dad. "Get a hole in one here and your name goes up on the Wall of Honor."

Judy took a swing and *wheee!* The ball shot up the ramp.

The ball flew over the shipwreck. The ball sailed through the air and landed with a *kerplunk*. But it didn't plop in the pond this time.

"HEY!"

It crash-landed, *splash*-landed, dead center in the middle of Stink's root-beer float!

"Vol-ca-no!" yelled Stink as root-beer float erupted and oozed all over.

"It's a sinker, Stinker!" called Judy.

"Hole in one!" called Dad.

"Sorry about the root-beer bath, Stinkerbell."

"What's the final score, Dad?" Stink asked.

"Oh, I was supposed to keep score?"

"Dad, no way! The Orange Crush squashed The Purple Putter!"

"You may have won the *goony-golf game,* Stink," said Judy, "but I used my *left hand* all day."

Ding-ding-ding-ding-ding! Just then, a bell rang. A man in a goony-golf shirt came running. "That's the wildest hole-in-one shot I've ever seen. This young lady gets her name on the High-Flying, Purple-People-Eater Hole-in-One Wall of Honor. And a free root-beer float!"

"For real?" Judy squealed.

Dad put his arms around them both. "My two silly southpaws."

"Live life left!" yelled Stink.

"Love laf leaf!" yelled Judy.

Check out the other
JUDY MOODY AND FRIENDS books!

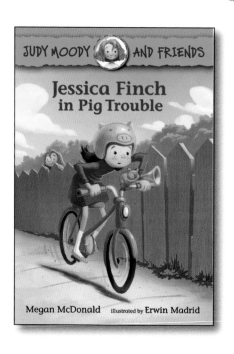

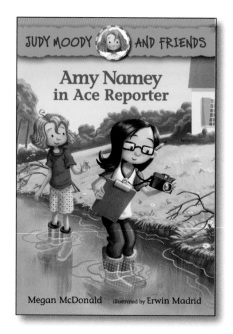

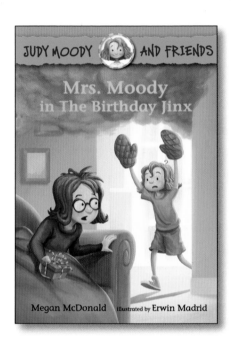

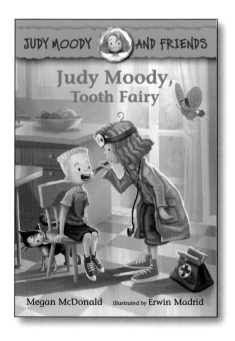